My Mommy Medicine

Written by Edwidge Danticat
Illustrated by Shannon Wright

Roaring Brook Press
New York

For Nara —E.D.

For my parents, Kevin and Diann Wright —S.W.

Text copyright © 2019 by Edwidge Danticat
Illustrations copyright © 2019 by Shannon Wright
Published by Roaring Brook Press
Roaring Brook Press is a division of Holtzbrinck Publishing Holdings Limited Partnership
175 Fifth Avenue, New York, NY 10010
mackids.com
All rights reserved

Library of Congress Control Number: 2018944877

ISBN: 978-1-250-14091-3

Our books may be purchased in bulk for promotional, educational, or business use.
Please contact your local bookseller or the Macmillan Corporate and Premium Sales Department
at (800) 221-7945 ext. 5442 or by e-mail at MacmillanSpecialMarkets@macmillan.com.

First edition 2019
Book design by Christina Dacanay
Printed in China by Hung Hing Off-set Printing Co. Ltd., Heshan City, Guangdong Province

10 9 8 7 6 5 4 3 2 1

Whenever I am sick,
or just feel kind of gloomy or sad,
I can always count
on my Mommy Medicine.

Sometimes it's a kiss so loud
it reminds me of a French horn at Mardi Gras.

Or a hug so warm and tight
it feels like wearing my
toastiest pajamas
on a cool cool night.

Sometimes it's a cuddly nose rub
or a massage that tickles.

Or a menthol back rub . . .
so minty it fills up
my whole room.

Sometimes it's fruity popsicles. Kiwi, watermelon.
Or just plain old vanilla ice cream will do.

Sometimes it's tea—ginger, cinnamon,
or peppermint.

Or even better, hot chocolate! Full of misty,
foamy milk that looks like clouds or angel wings.

Or soup—pea, chicken, or squash.
I love squash! It's like sunshine in a bowl.

Sometimes it's bubbles,
the kind of bubbles you blow,
or catch, or sink into in the tub.

Sometimes it's a card game,
Uno or Crazy Eights,
or maybe chess or dominos,
or if I'm feeling up to it . . .

a piggyback ride.

Or an indoor horseshoe toss.

Sometimes it's a whispered prayer,
just before nodding off at nap time.

And sometimes it's a song at bedtime,
when Brother John is sleeping,
and the Itsy Bitsy Spider
is climbing up a waterspout,
and little stars are twinkling,
and I'm Mommy's sunshine and she is mine,
and we make each other happy.
Even when skies are gray.

Sometimes it's a silly dance
we make up ourselves,
a dance that works
even if you have to stay in bed.

And sometimes it's a story where we sail off on a great big adventure to a faraway land where everyone is in trouble and only Mommy and I (and, of course, a little magic) can save the whole entire world.

Or we watch a favorite movie that
makes us laugh and laugh and laugh,
and makes us cry a little too.

Or we cover our castle box
with all the drawings we've made.

And sometimes it's just plain old sitting up,
Mommy and me, propped up against my favorite pillow,
while watching my ceiling's glow-in-the-dark stars flicker,
making our own sky.

Sometimes it's even *actual* medicine,
which might taste yummy
or YUCKY.

But nothing will ever

EVER

take the place of

My Mommy Medicine.

Author's Note

I am the mother of two daughters—Mira, thirteen, and Leila, ten—and ever since they were little, whenever they weren't feeling well, I would lavish them with what we called "Mommy Medicine." These were acts of comfort that they found soothing, reassuring, and somewhat healing. The idea for this book came from many sick days spent at home with Mira and Leila, and before them, my niece and nephew, Nadira and Ezekiel. Mommy in this case can be, yes, a mother, but also an aunt, a dad, a grandma, grandpa, a guardian or caretaker, or anyone who has to keep little ones entertained while they're not feeling well. Sometimes when I have to travel while my daughters are sick, I tell them that whoever is staying with them—usually their dad and/or grandmother—is going to give them some great care, plus some Mommy Medicine. Mommy Medicine is based on shared affection and a strong desire to make someone you love feel better.

What's your Mommy Medicine?